Good and Perfect Gifts

Barry Moser

Good and Perfect Gifts

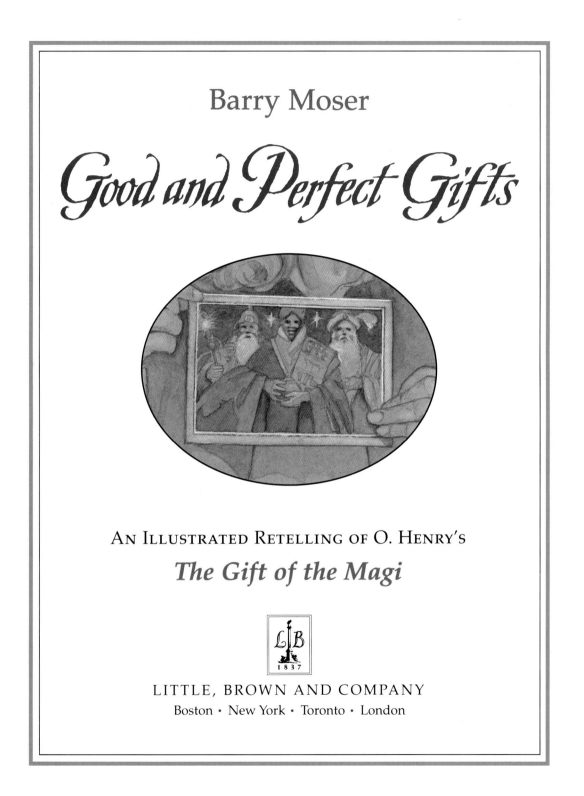

AN ILLUSTRATED RETELLING OF O. HENRY'S

The Gift of the Magi

LITTLE, BROWN AND COMPANY
Boston · New York · Toronto · London

First Edition

Library of Congress Cataloging-in-Publication Data

Moser, Barry.
  Good and perfect gifts : an illustrated retelling of O. Henry's The gift of the
Magi / Barry Moser.—1st ed.
      p.   cm.
  Summary: Based on the classic story in which a husband and wife sacrifice
treasured possessions in order to buy each other Christmas presents.
  ISBN 0-316-58543-2
  [1. Gifts—Fiction.   2. Christmas—Fiction.]   I. Henry, O., 1862–1910.
Gift of the Magi.   II. Title.
PZ7.M8469357Go   1997
[Fic]—dc20   94-39168

10 9 8 7 6 5 4 3 2

IM

Published simultaneously in Canada by Little, Brown & Company (Canada) Limited

Printed in Singapore

In memory of my grandmother,
Hattie Evie Whitten Moser, 1882–1954,
a fine seamstress and giver of good and perfect gifts

Every good and perfect gift is from above.

—James 1:17

IT WAS THE Sunday before Christmas. Rebecca Vondell was teaching her Sunday school class down at the Calvary Methodist Church, like she did every Sunday. This week she was teaching the story of the Nativity—the one found in the Gospel according to Matthew, where he tells about the three kings from the East who came to Bethlehem to see the baby Jesus.

She held up a picture for the children to see.

"Miz Vondell, did they have names?" Everett Cullen asked.

"None that're in the Bible," Rebecca replied. "But speaking of names—you know what else? The wise men are not always called wise men either."

"They're not?" Hettie Schumate asked.

"Nope, unh-uh. Some people call them Magi."

"Magi? How do you spell that, Miz Vondell?" Jo Annie Belk asked.

"*M . . . a . . . g . . . i,*" Rebecca answered.

"If you put a *c* on the end, it'd spell *magic,* wouldn't it?" Jo Annie said, pushing her glasses up on her nose.

"Why, darlin', I 'spect it would."

Then Rebecca went on and told them about how the wise men got on their camels and rode all the way from Persia or someplace like that, having nothing to go by but a real bright star way off in the eastern sky. From that night on, she said, folks had always called that star the Star of Bethlehem, and she told the children that it had never been seen again, not ever—not even up to right now.

Then Clyde Schumate said, "Well, if they wuz a-followin' a star, how'd they know where they wuz a-goin' in the daylight, Mizzzz Vondell?"

"I couldn't rightly say, Clyde," Rebecca replied, annoyed at the way he said *Miz*. "Maybe they just rested up and slept during the day."

The word *day* was barely out of her mouth when Clyde asked, "An' you said the star wuz in the eastern sky. . . . Well, wouldn't the star be in the *western* sky if'n they wuz a-travelin' from the East? Huh? Wouldn't it?"

"Clyde!" Rebecca scolded. "You just stop that foolishness right now."

Clyde folded his arms across his chest and scrunched down in his seat. Rebecca gave him a stern look and continued with the lesson. "You know, class," she said, "the whole reason for the wise men coming all that way and going to all that trouble was just to bring some real nice presents to a little bitty baby they didn't even know."

"What kinda presents, Miz Vondell?" Ro Berta Tyler asked.

"Well, Ro Berta," Rebecca said as she held up a picture of the Nativity, "the Bible tells us that they brought gold and frankincense and myrrh."

"What's frankin-since?" interrupted Clyde.

"What's murh?" echoed Everett Cullen.

"They're both kinda like perfume, aren't they, Miz Vondell?" Jo Annie Belk asked.

"I think that's right, Jo Annie," Rebecca answered.

"Well, what's a baby need perfume for, anyhow?" Clyde asked.

"I don't know, honey—it's just what the Good Book says."

"My mama says babies are nicest when they've been powdered up an' smell real good."

"I 'spect that's so, Ro Berta."

"Shoot," Clyde said, "it seems like if them wise men wuz all that wise, they'da brought 'em sumpthin' they could really use— like a buggy for their donkey to pull, or sumpthin'."

"You might be right, Clyde. I reckon gifts ought to be useful, and something like a buggy sure would've made that sweet little family's trip a lot more comfortable, wouldn't it have?"

She held up another picture, one showing the babe in the manger.

After Sunday school, Rebecca met her husband, Fenton, down in the Fellowship Room and then went to the eleven o'clock church service and listened to their preacher, Rev. Orval Rule, preach. The sermon was supposed to be about the *real* meaning of Christmas, but Reverend Rule got off on how much God needs money and how he thought everybody ought to give extra offerings when the plates got passed around this morning. He never did get back to what he thought Christmas really meant. He passed the plates twice, and by the time he got through preaching and let church out, it was pretty near one o'clock in the afternoon.

Rebecca and Fenton took the shortcut across the old suspension bridge and hurried home because Rebecca was worrying that her Sunday dinner might be ruined, but it wasn't.

They lived in a trailer over in the Stoney Creek Mobile Home Park on Route 30. The Vondell trailer was at the end of the first drive, tucked up into the side of the ridge. It was comfortable and quiet, except for the noise of the whining tires of the few semis that still used Route 30. Their cat, Dinah, sat in the window, waiting for them.

Fenton was an auto mechanic. He worked for Joe Willie Cotter, whose auto repair shop, the Junction Garage, was part filling station, part grocery store, and part restaurant. They called the little restaurant the Catfish Junction and fixed the best fried catfish and hush puppies and coleslaw this side of Chattanooga.

Business at Junction Garage had fallen off a lot lately, and Fenton was behind three weeks pay. On the weekends he did

rough carpentry with Hoyt and Wesley Gann and Wesley's two oldest boys, Jack and Nate. Most weekends he could earn a little extra money swinging a hammer, but right now, it being winter and so many people being out of work and all, there wasn't much building going on and Fenton wasn't making anything extra. The money he had saved up from his carpentry work had only been enough to put Rebecca's Christmas present on layaway at Stevenson's Antique Shop—a fine old handmade chest that he thought would be the perfect thing for Rebecca to keep her mother's quilt in. Miz Stevenson was a real nice lady and had offered to let him take it and just owe her the money, but Fenton had declined her offer because he didn't want to give Rebecca a present that wasn't paid for.

Rebecca had a day job as a hairdresser down at the Hair We Are Style Shoppe. She worked for a lady named Floye Mae Richards, but there didn't seem to be much more work for hairdressers these days than there was for carpenters. So Rebecca filled in for the waitresses down at the Catfish Junction whenever she could, and sometimes—on Mondays when Miz Richards closed her shop—she got called in to dust the merchandise on the shelves of the hardware store. But nothing did much good.

When she wasn't working for Miz Richards or waiting tables or dusting merchandise, Rebecca spent as much time as she could down at the church making quilts—it was the only place she had access to that was big enough for her quilt frames. Rebecca had learned quilting from her mother, Evie Springer. She'd passed over just this past spring. Her name was Evangeline Estelle Springer, and she was one of the best quilters in that part of the state. Rebecca used her mother's patterns—mostly the religious themes like Tree of Life and Forbidden Fruit—but Rebecca's own personal favorite was Star of Bethlehem. She sold her quilts at a mountain crafts shop on the outskirts of town on Route 411 heading over towards Knoxville, but she hadn't sold one recently, and she was getting uneasy now because Christmas was this coming Friday and what she had saved up from her pay and tip money wasn't nearly enough to buy Fenton's present with.

Then, late Christmas Eve morning, Rebecca acted on an idea she had been thinking about for some time. She threw on her jacket and scarf and ran down to the pay phone at the corner. She pinched the collar of her jacket up under her chin with her free hand as she looked up Judge Wycuff's number in the telephone directory, dialed it, and waited for somebody to answer.

"Miz Wycuff?"

"Yes."

"Miz Wycuff, this is Rebecca Vondell. You remember me? I was Rebecca Springer before I got married."

"Why, of course, sugar, I remember you. I was a big admirer of your mama's quilts, God bless her sweet soul."

"Well, Miz Wycuff, that's why I'm calling. Do you remember that quilt of my mama's you wanted to buy two years ago at the county fair . . . the one that took first prize?"

"I surely do. It was such a beautiful thing, that quilt. Your mama wouldn't sell it to me 'cause she was going to give it to you for a wedding present, as I recall. Isn't that right?"

"Yes, ma'am, that's right. And that's why I'm calling. Would you still be interested in buying it?"

"Why, sugar, of course I would. But why in the world would you want to sell it?"

"I need the money to buy my husband's Christmas present."

"Well . . . okay . . . ," Miz Wycuff said hesitantly, "but only if you're absolutely positive you want to sell it."

"Yes, ma'am, I'm sure. But," Rebecca added, "if I bring it over right now, can you pay me for it? I really need the money today."

"Sure, honey, you hurry on over right now. I'll have the money waiting for you when you get here."

"Yes'm. And thank you, Miz Wycuff. I'm on my way."

Rebecca hung up and hurried back to the trailer to pack up her mother's quilt. When she took it out of the closet, its faint familiar smell broke her heart, but she was sure she was doing the right thing. She put the quilt in a wagon and walked the five miles over to the Wycuff place to sell her mother's quilt.

Then she walked back into town pulling her empty wagon. She was headed to Chalmers' Hardware Store to buy Fenton a steel tool chest for his tools. Fenton was real particular about his tools. He wouldn't buy anything but the best, and had been buying and collecting tools from the Snap-on salesman for three or four years now.

Every Wednesday about one o'clock, the salesman, Dave Marchand, pulled his big white Snap-on truck up to the Junction Garage, and Fenton bought one or two new tools whenever he could afford it. Rebecca laughed a little to herself as she walked, remembering the time she saw the Snap-on truck pull up in front of the garage, and Fenton and all the other mechanics dropping whatever they were doing and gathering around the truck shopping for new tools. They reminded her of a bunch of little boys running around the ding-dong man buying ice cream and Popsicles. Last year Fenton bought a real expensive half-inch-drive ratchet-and-socket set on credit from Mr. Marchand. It took him nearly the whole year to pay for it, and by then, somebody had already stolen one of his ratchets. The tool chest Rebecca was going to buy was the one she had seen in the window of Chalmers' Hardware last week. She just knew that it would be *the* absolute perfect gift. With that, she thought, Fenton could lock up his tools, good and safe.

Rebecca cheered up considerably when she got to the hardware store and saw the tool chest still sitting in the front window. It was going to be a real good Christmas after all, she thought. Mr. Chalmers, the owner, even gave her a discount because it was

Christmas Eve and getting near to closing time—and besides, when he was taking it out of the window, he put a little scratch in it, although it was just a tiny one you wouldn't hardly notice.

Mr. Chalmers put the chest into a heavy cardboard box and wrapped it up in brown paper, but Rebecca thought it just looked too plain like that, so she went across the street to the ten-cent store and bought some ribbons to decorate it with. She wished the sales clerk a Merry Christmas and then went next door to Will Haggard's grocery store and bought a stewing chicken, a can of mashed pumpkin, and a bag of Christmas candy to put in a bowl tomorrow morning. She was going to fix chicken and dumplings and pumpkin pie for Christmas dinner.

When she got back to the hardware store, Mr. Chalmers was turning the lights off and talking to Randall Schumate, who had come in looking for some spark plugs. Clyde and Hettie Schumate were looking out the front window and saw Rebecca coming. Clyde opened the door for her and held it.

"Why thank you, Clyde. That's awful nice of you."

"Welcome," Clyde said shyly.

"Hey, Mr. Schumate," Rebecca said. "Merry Christmas."

"Merry Christmas, Rebecca," he replied.

"Now listen, little lady," Mr. Chalmers said to Rebecca, "it's getting too dark for you to be walking home a-pullin' that little old wagon of yours. We'll just put everything in the back of my truck, and I'll give you a lift home."

"That's awful sweet of you Mr. Chalmers, but—"

"No *buts*, now, Rebecca. It's Christmas Eve and it's the least I can do."

"Well, thank you an awful lot. I do appreciate it. This way I'll get home before Fenton does for sure, and I can hide his present so he won't see it till tomorrow." She turned to the Schumates and said, "Good night, y'all. And Clyde . . . ," she said as she took the bag of candy out of her grocery bag and gave it to him, "you and Hettie have a real Merry Christmas!"

Christmas morning came and with it rain. The sound of the rain peppering down on the roof made Rebecca want to stay in bed and snuggle up warm with her husband. But she didn't. She got up, pulled the covers up around Fenton, got dressed, and went to her little hallway-like kitchen and started fixing their Christmas dinner.

While she was standing there making the pie crust and rolling out the dumplings, Fenton got out of bed, sneaked up behind her, and surprised her with a real tight hug. He took her by the elbow and pointed towards their tiny sitting room and said, "Darlin,' you just gotta come on right this minute 'cause there's somethin' in there I'm just dyin' to show you and I just can't wait another dad-blamed second."

Rebecca laughed and giggled a little and said, "Okay . . . but you'll have to wait till I wash my hands first."

She was still drying her hands when she stepped into the sitting room and caught sight of the fine polished chest gleaming near the little pine tree that they had decorated last night. She knew immediately what it was intended for. A brim of tears formed in her eyes as she absentmindedly kept drying her hands even though they were already dry. Fenton saw a tear pearl down her cheek. He went to her and held her in his arms and asked her if she was crying because she was missing her mama.

"Well, Fenton . . . ," Rebecca said, drying her eyes with the towel. "Yes, I do miss Mother. I miss her something awful. This is the first Christmas I've ever spent without her . . . but that's not why I'm crying, not really."

"Well then, what in the world's the matter, sweetheart?" Fenton asked.

"The chest is for Mother's quilt, isn't it?"

"Yes. I thought it was just right for it. Go get it—you'll see. It'll fit perfect."

"I can't go get it, Fenton."

"How come?"

"Because I went and sold it to Miz Wycuff."

Fenton was dumbfounded. "Let me show you why," she said. And then, without another word, Rebecca went over to the corner of the tiny little room and lifted the cloth that was covering a card table and showed him his present, all tied up with brown wrapping paper and red ribbons.

Fenton was caught completely by surprise because there was already a present under the tree with his name on it, but all it was was a decoy—an empty box Rebecca wrapped up just to fool him and keep him from snooping around and finding something she didn't want him to find.

She started to drag the heavy package out from under the card table.

"Don't strain yourself, honey. Let me get it for you," Fenton said as he stepped around her and lifted his gift and set it down next to the tree. "Wow! It's heavy!" he said with a big smile. Then he sat down cross-legged in the middle of the floor, undid the ribbons, and removed the brown paper wrapping.

When he saw the printing on the outside of the box, he knew exactly what was inside, and he started to laugh.

"What in the world are you laughing at, Fenton Vondell?" Rebecca wanted to know. "Don't you like your present?"

"Oh, yes. YES!" Fenton said. "It's just that . . ."

"Just what? What's the matter?"

Fenton stared silently out the rain-streaked window for a minute. Then, in a soft voice, he said, "Honey, I sold all my tools."

"You did what?"

"I sold all my tools back to Mr. Marchand."

"Well, why in the world did you do that, Fenton?"

"To buy you that chest there for your mama's quilt!"

They sat snuggled together for a little while, listening to the gentle rain and Dinah's soft purring. Then Fenton said, "Listen, sugar, I'll have me a set of new tools in no time—a set bigger an' better than my old ones. And just think, I'll have this fine tool chest you give me to put them in. Sweetheart, it's such a wonderful present! The best tool chest in the entire world—I just know it is! An' Rebecca, I promise you something: I'm gonna work hard—I'm gonna work *real* hard—an' I'll put some money aside whenever I can . . . an' then one day I'll go to Miz Wycuff and try to buy back your mama's quilt for you."

Rebecca got up slowly and touched Fenton on the back of his head. He looked up at her just as she said, "We'll see, honey. We'll see. . . . Right now I gotta go check on the chicken."

When she took the lid off the pot, the steam lifted the aroma of their Christmas dinner into the chill air. As she was setting the table, Rebecca thought about the lesson she'd taught in Sunday school last Sunday. She thought about her mother's quilt and what a beautiful wedding present it had been. And as she was putting her pumpkin pie in the oven, she remembered a verse from the Epistle of James, something about good and perfect gifts—it might make a good Sunday school lesson for this coming week—she'd think about it. Then she called out, "Fenton, dinner's just about on the table—come on, now, before it gets cold."